Welcome to
Hopscotch Hill School!
In Miss Sparks's class,
you will make friends
with children just like you.
They love school,
and they love to learn!
Keep an eye out for Razzi,
the class pet rabbit.
He may be anywhere!
See if you can spot him
as you read the story.

Welcome!
Student of the Week!
Miss Sparks
Skylar
Razzi
Logan
Hallie

Avery
Spencer
Nathan
Gwen
Lindy
Delaney
Connor

Published by Pleasant Company Publications

For information, address:
Book Editor, Pleasant Company Publications, 8400 Fairway Place, P.O. Box 620998, Middleton, WI 53562.

Visit our Web site at **americangirl.com**

Printed in China
03 04 05 06 07 08 09 10 C&C 10 9 8 7 6 5 4 3 2

Cataloging-in-Publication data available from the Library of Congress

American Girl
Bright, Shiny Skylar
by Valerie Tripp illustrated by Joy Allen

The Happiest Girl

Skylar was the happiest girl
in Miss Sparks's class.
Bright and early
on the second day of school,
Skylar zoomed into the classroom.
Skylar said, "Hi, everybody!"
"Hi, Skylar!" said the children.
Miss Sparks said, "Hello, Skylar.
You look bright and shiny today."
"Thanks!" said Skylar.
Skylar rose up on her tiptoes.
She spun all around.
All the children smiled.
Skylar was wearing
her favorite hair clips.
They looked like shiny stars.

Skylar knew that Miss Sparks
liked shiny stars too.
Miss Sparks had sparkles
on her eyeglasses
that were shiny like stars.
Miss Sparks said, "Skylar,
please put your lunch
in your cubby.
Then please be seated
at your desk."

"Okay!" said Skylar.

Skylar scooted to the

back of the room.

She put her lunch in her cubby.

On the way back to her desk,

Skylar stopped.

She saw that Nathan

had his lunchbox on his desk.

Nathan was looking at the

superhero on his lunchbox.

"Hey, Nathan," Skylar said.
"You are supposed to put
your lunch in your cubby."
Nathan did not say a word.
"Don't worry, Nathan," said Skylar.
"I will put your lunch
in your cubby for you."
Nathan put his hand
on his lunchbox.

Skylar tugged a little bit
and took it away from him.
She zipped to the back
of the room.
Skylar could read
so it was easy for her
to find Nathan's cubby.
Skylar put Nathan's lunchbox
in his cubby.
"Boys and girls," said Miss Sparks.
"It is time to sit
at your desks."
Skylar went to her desk
and sat down.
Just then Skylar saw
rainbows on the walls!

The rainbows were made
by the sun shining through
the prisms by the windows.
Skylar jumped up from her seat.
She flew over to the wall.
She just had to touch the rainbows!

Miss Sparks said, "Boys and girls.
I like the way most of you
sat down when I asked you to.
I will wait for the rest of you
to be seated now."
Skylar scurried back to her desk.
Miss Sparks went to the piano.
She said, "I am going to sing
'America the Beautiful.'
Listen to me or sing along
if you know the words."
Skylar was so happy!
She knew the song by heart.
Her older sister had taught her
all the words when they
played school at home.

Skylar tilted her head back
and sang, “Oh beautiful
for spacious skies . . .”
Skylar saw that the ceiling
was painted blue with clouds.
It was beautiful,
just like the sky in the song!
Skylar jumped up from her seat.
“Hey, look everybody!” shouted Skylar.

She pointed to the ceiling.
"We have a sky in our classroom."
Everybody was mixed up.
Some children stopped singing.
Some children kept on singing.
Then Miss Sparks stopped
playing the piano.
"Skylar," said Miss Sparks.
"Please do not interrupt."
"Okay," said Skylar.
She sat down.
Miss Sparks and
the children went back to singing.
Skylar sang the words
nice and fast and loud:
"From sea to shining sea."

Bounciness

Lots of things about school
were easy for Skylar,
like reading, writing, and math.
In fact, there was only one thing
that was hard for Skylar.
It was hard for Skylar
to stay quietly in her seat.
Skylar just had to jump up
and call out answers.
When Miss Sparks asked,
"What day is it today?"
Skylar jumped up and called out,
"It's Wednesday!"

"Oh, Skylar," said Miss Sparks.
"I like the way you are so
enthusiastic! But please
remember our class rule.
Raise your hand if you
have something to say."
"Okay!" said Skylar.
Miss Sparks began to ask,
"How many days until . . ."
"Oh!" exclaimed Skylar.
She raised her hand
high above her head
and waved it.
"I know! I know!" Skylar said.
"Miss Sparks!
Me! Me! Call on me."

Then Skylar couldn’t hold

the answer in any longer.

She jumped up out of her seat.

“Two!” Skylar exclaimed.

“The answer is two.

There are two days

until the weekend.”

Suddenly the whole room was quiet.

Everyone was looking at Skylar.

Skylar realized she had done it again.
She had jumped up out of her seat.
She had called out the answer.
The sparkles on Miss Sparks's
eyeglasses were not shiny at all.
"Skylar," said Miss Sparks.
"I am afraid you did not listen
to the whole question.
I was going to ask how many days
until the end of the month."
"Oh," said Skylar. She sank
down like a popped balloon.

Miss Sparks called on Hallie.

"There are five days until

the end of the month,"

said Hallie.

"Thank you, Hallie,"

said Miss Sparks.

Skylar was a smart girl.

She could see

that her bounciness

was getting her into trouble.

When she jumped out of her seat

and shouted out answers,

Miss Sparks was not pleased.

When Skylar jumped up

and showed the other children

what to do, they did not like it.

Skylar wanted to stop
being so bouncy.
She wanted to teach
herself to stay put.
Skylar had an idea.
She made herself
a long chain of rubber bands.
She looped the chain
around her waist and
connected it to her chair.
Skylar hoped that the rubber bands
would hold her in her seat
if she jumped up.

But during math

Gwen made a mistake

at the chalkboard.

Gwen wrote 3 + 2 = 6.

Skylar jumped up out of her seat to

go fix Gwen's mistake.

Boing! went the rubber bands.

They broke.

They did not stop Skylar at all.

The next day Skylar made
a belt of paper clips
to hold her in her chair.
But during story time
Skylar jumped up out of her seat.
She wanted to point
to the cow in the picture.
Poing! The belt broke.
Paper clips flew all over.
"Hey," joked Spencer.
"It's raining paper clips in here!"

The next day Skylar put
lots of sticky tape
on the seat of her pants.
She hoped the tape would
hold her in her chair.
But when the class was drawing,
Skylar saw Razzi hiding
behind the reading tub.
Skylar jumped up to get Razzi.
The tape made a big ripping noise.
The noise scared Razzi,
but the tape did not stop Skylar.
Skylar was very discouraged.
She was so bouncy that
nothing could keep her
in her seat. Nothing.

Starring Skylar

One day Miss Sparks
had a special smile.
"Boys and girls," she said.
"Our class has been asked
to paint a mural
for the lunchroom.
The mural will be a surprise
for your parents when they
visit on Back to School Night."
"Oooh," said the children.
Skylar was excited.
She knew what a mural was.

A mural was
a long, long picture.
The children decided that
a mural of the sky would look nice
in the lunchroom.
Miss Sparks unrolled
a long, long sheet of paper.
She put the paper on the floor.
For the next few days
everyone worked very hard.

Some children painted a blue sky.

Some children glued

white cotton balls onto

the blue sky to look like clouds.

Some children painted a rainy sky.

They painted gray clouds.

The clouds had silver glitter glue

falling from them.

The glitter glue looked just like rain.

Skylar was helping to paint

a rainbow.

Skylar knew all about rainbows.

She saw that Spencer was

making a mistake.

He was painting

the rainbow blue

where it should have been red.

"Hey, Spencer!" said Skylar.

"That's wrong!"

Skylar jumped up to

go to Spencer.

Crash! Splash! Oh no!

Skylar knocked over

a pail of water

full of paintbrushes.

The water spilled

all over the mural.

The blue sky was ruined.

The cotton ball clouds

were ruined.

The rain cloud was ruined.

The silver glitter glue rain was ruined.

Some of the children

were so sad that they cried.

Skylar cried too.

"I'm sorry!" Skylar wailed.

But it was too late.

Everyone's hard work was wasted.

There was not enough time
to start over again.
Skylar had never felt
so sad in her whole life.
She was the saddest girl
in Miss Sparks's class
and in the whole school
and in the whole world.
All the children went home.
Skylar stayed behind
to clean up the water
she had spilled.
"Oh, Miss Sparks," said Skylar.
"I don't want to be
so bouncy.
I wish I could change.

I have tried to change.

But I can not."

Miss Sparks smiled.

She said, "You are my

bright, shiny Skylar.

The real sky changes,

and you will too,

with time and trying."

Skylar thought about the sky
and how it changed.
Suddenly Skylar had
a bright, shiny idea.
The next day
Skylar raised her hand.
When Miss Sparks called on her,
Skylar told the class
about her idea.
Skylar said,
"Instead of a day sky,
we could paint a night sky."
Everyone loved Skylar's idea!
Some of the children
went to work
painting the ruined mural black.

Some of the children sat
at their desks cutting
stars out of paper.
Everyone worked hard.
But no one worked as hard as Skylar.
Skylar put sticky glitter glue
on the paper stars
to make them shiny.
It took a very long time.

The sticky glitter glue
helped Skylar remember
to stick to her work.
She did not jump up
from her seat once,
not once all morning.
When the stars were finished,
Skylar and the other children
glued them to the mural.
Skylar saw that some of
the children were gluing
the stars too close together.
But she did not make a peep.
She just stuck to her work
sticking the stars
on the mural.

When all the stars were glued on,
Miss Sparks and Skylar held up
the mural to show the class.
"Oooh," said all the children.
The mural of the night sky
was beautiful!
The glitter glue made the stars
sparkle and shine
just like real stars.

Skylar smiled.

She was proud of the way

she had stuck to her work.

The sticky stars had shown

Skylar that she could change.

Just like changing the mural,

changing herself would take

time and hard work.

But now Skylar knew

that she could do it.

Nathan pointed at Skylar.

"Look," said Nathan.

"Skylar has sticky glitter glue

stuck on her fingers, on her face,

and in her hair!"

All the children smiled.

Skylar rose up on her tiptoes
and spun all around
to make the glitter glue sparkle.
All the children laughed.
Miss Sparks said,
"That's our bright,
shiny Skylar!"

Dear Parents . . .

B*ounce, bounce, bounce* . . . Doesn't it seem that the more energy your child uses, the more she seems to have? Of course, she needs that enviable energy at school. It fuels her enthusiasm for learning and for meeting new challenges. But just like bright, shiny Skylar, your child will find that to be a bright, shiny scholar, she'll have to focus her energy. And that can be hard. It's hard to sit still at her desk when she's itching to get up and go. It's hard to listen to her teacher when fascinating books and games in the classroom call out to her. It's even hard to slow down and get to know the other children when there are so many other fascinating things she just *has* to do.

How can you help your perpetual motion machine learn self-control? How can you help her be observant, attentive, and aware of others? Bounciness can't be calmed overnight. But just as Miss Sparks tells Skylar, change will come with "time and trying." The fun activities on the following pages can help, too!

On the Move

Your child greets the world of school with her arms wide open. Her body's alive with physical energy. Her mind's alert and full of ideas she can't wait to express. That enthusiasm will serve her well as a student—if she can focus it. Here are some ways you can help your child begin to take charge of her energy so that she can charge into school as a winner:

- Many children are *kinesthetic learners,* which means they need to move in order to learn. Whenever possible, make learning an active experience for your child. Ask her to act out spelling words or use blocks to show you what she's learned in math. Let her be **poetry in motion** as she recites jingles or rhymes she has heard. Encourage her to act out scenes from stories or to draw while you read to her.

- *Immediately.* That's when your child wants to touch, try, and explore everything in the classroom. To help her be less impulsive, play the **stoplight game** at home. Before you give her the green light to have a snack or start a game, tell her she must do a yellow light step and a red light step. Make the steps lively, like hopping on one foot or singing a song.

- If your little dynamo has a hard time staying put at her desk at school, teach her some ways to **release pent-up energy.** She can do the "lemon squeeze" by clenching her fists and then relaxing them. She can take "balloon breaths" by filling her lungs like a balloon and then slowly letting air out. Be sure she knows lots of run-around games to play at recess, too, so that she can enjoy using her energy.

- It may be very hard for your child to wait for the teacher to call on her when she's exploding to express herself! Helping her learn to wait begins at home. When friends or family are gathered, make a game out of **taking turns talking.** Go clockwise around the dinner table or the living room, and give everyone a chance to speak without being interrupted. Your child will find it easier to wait if she knows she'll have a turn to be heard.

All Ears

Is your child a charming chatterbox? Most children between the ages of 4 and 6 are. They're terrific talkers and super storytellers, full of fascinating observations and curious questions about the world around them. But while they're very good at talking, they're usually not so good at listening. Here are some ways to help your child "tune in":

- **Draw as a duo,** back-to-back, so that you can't see each other's work. Take turns giving directions about what to draw. Let your child begin. If she says, "I'm drawing a red house," you draw one, too. Your turn is next. If you say, "I'm drawing a dog," your child should draw a dog, too. After a few turns, compare drawings. Do your eyes see what your ears heard?

- Turn driving time into listening time. Teach your child a song, an old saying, a jingle, or a short poem. Recite it line by line, and ask your child to repeat it back to you. Or play **Simon Says.** Say, "Simon says touch your nose," or "Simon says knock three times on the window." Slip in some commands that don't start with "Simon says" to see how well your child is listening.

- Give your child **choosy clues.** If she's trying to decide which sweater to wear, give her clues to help her choose. Say, "I have white stripes, buttons shaped like bunnies, and blue sleeves." If she's trying to decide which book to read together, say, "My cover is blue. I'm about a mouse. I rhyme." If she's trying to choose a snack, say, "I'm in the refrigerator, in the fruit drawer, and I'm red." Give her cheers if she uses her ears!

- When you **read aloud** to your child, stop from time to time. Remark on the action you just read about. Ask your child, "Why do you think that happened? What do you think will happen next?" You'll keep her "all ears" as you read!

Fair Feelings

To understand how someone else feels, we have to stop and look as well as listen. Learning to read body language and facial expressions is as important for your child as learning to read books. You can help her grow to be an observant, thoughtful friend to her classmates. As she builds compassion for others, she will learn to better express her own emotions, too.

- **Use the illustrations** in *Bright, Shiny Skylar* as a jumping-off place. Talk about how Skylar's bouncy behavior affected others. For example, point to the picture on page 10 and ask your child, "How do you think Nathan felt?" and "How do you know he felt that way?" Ask your child if she has ever felt like Nathan. Then turn to page 35 and ask your child, "How does Nathan feel now?" Ask her about happy and sad times she has had at school.

- Cuddle up with your child and look at the faces of people in newspaper comics or magazine photographs. See if your child can name the emotion behind each expression. Ask, "Why do you think the person feels that way?" Encourage your child to **make up a story**—sad or funny—to explain why.

- Words are the tools your child needs to express her emotions. Make a list of **feeling words,** and take turns acting out the words with your child. Use simple words such as *sad, happy, worried, angry, frightened, excited, surprised, shy, disappointed, confused,* and *hopeful.* Talk about times your child has felt these emotions. Reassure her that all feelings are fair; it is how she acts on them that matters.

- Bright, shiny Skylar learned that she *could* change if she tried. Talk to your child about the ways she has **grown and changed.** Does she remember to say "thank you" without being prompted? Is she kinder about sharing her things with others? If some improvements are still works in progress, remind her that change takes "time and trying." Praise her efforts, and encourage her not to give up.

Bright, Shiny Skylar and the activities that follow the story were developed with guidance from the Hopscotch Hill School advisory board:

Dominic Gullo is a professor and the program chair of Early Childhood Education at the University of Wisconsin, Milwaukee. He is a member of the governing board of the National Association for the Education of Young Children, and he is a consultant to school districts across the country in the areas of early childhood education, curriculum, and assessment.

Margaret Jensen has taught beginning reading for 32 years and is currently a math resource teacher in the Madison Metropolitan School District, Wisconsin. She has served on committees for the International Reading Association and the Wisconsin State Reading Association, and has been president of the Madison Area Reading Council. She has presented at workshops and conferences in the areas of reading, writing, and children's literature.

Kim Miller is a school psychologist at Lowell Elementary in Madison, Wisconsin, where she works with children, parents, and teachers to help solve—and prevent—problems related to learning and adjustment to the classroom setting.

Virginia Pickerell has worked with teachers and parents as an educational consultant and counselor within the Madison Metropolitan School District. She has researched and presented workshops on topics such as learning processes, problem solving, and creativity. She is also a former director of Head Start.

Place
Stamp
Here

PO BOX 620497
MIDDLETON WI 53562-0497